# CEltIC TALES
## of the
## Strange

Joanne Asala

*Illustrated by Marlene Ekman*

Sterling Publishing Co., Inc.
New York

*For Fiach O'Byrne*
Until we meet again in the Land of Ever Young

Edited by Jeanette Green

**Library of Congress Cataloging-in-Publication Data**
Asala, Joanne.
    Celtic tales of the strange / Joanne Asala ; illustrated by
Marlene Ekman.
       p.     cm.
    Includes index.
    ISBN 0-8069-9671-4
    1. Occultism—Ireland.   2. Supernatural.   3. Spirits.   4. Ireland—
Religion.   I. Title.
BF1434.I73A72   1997
398.2'09415—dc21                        97-17802


1   3   5   7   9   10   8   6   4   2

Published by Sterling Publishing Company, Inc.
387 Park Avenue South, New York, N.Y. 10016
© 1997 by Joanne Asala
Distributed in Canada by Sterling Publishing
% Canadian Manda Group, One Atlantic Avenue, Suite 105
Toronto, Ontario, Canada M6K 3E7
Distributed in Great Britain and Europe by Cassell PLC
Wellington House, 125 Strand, London WC2R 0BB, England
Distributed in Australia by Capricorn Link (Australia) Pty Ltd.
P.O. Box 6651, Baulkham Hills, Business Centre, NSW 2153, Australia
*Manufactured in the United States of America*

Sterling ISBN 0-8069-9671-4

# Contents

# DEMONS & THE DARK OF THE SEA

# Son of the Waves

MANY HUNDREDS AND HUNDREDS of years ago, on a Saturday afternoon it was, a fisherman from Bantry was fishing in the deep waters of the Atlantic. Donagh O'Donovan his name was, and there was nothing he liked better than the solitude he found at sea, with the sun shining down on his head and the wind at his back.

The day was right fair, and fish were plentiful. Toward sundown Donagh felt a great tug on his line. "Why, it's quite a large fish, judging by the strength of it!" he thought. "It'll bring me enough money for a pint or two at O'Malley's and leave me with some coins to jingle in my pocket!"

He struggled to haul the fish onto the deck, and when he had it on board, his eyes nearly popped from their sockets. He had caught a real, live boy! His hair was as red as the flesh of a salmon, and his eyes as green as mist over the ocean. Gills opened and shut uselessly on the sides of his neck. The hook was stuck firmly in his cheek.

Donagh was very proud of his catch. Who wouldn't be? "The money I'll make showing such a marvel!" he exclaimed. "People will pay good silver to see such a sight!" The boy ran and hid behind a pile of nets and stayed there until the fisherman pulled into the harbor.

Donagh took him home. "Maura!" he called. "Come look at what I caught today!" His wife, wiping her hands on her apron, came out to the yard to see what her husband was shouting about. But as soon as he set the boy down on the ground, the boy raced into the cottage and hid under the bed. No one could get him to come out, neither with coaxing nor with offers of food. Even

Donagh's eldest son, who threatened the sea child with a pitchfork, couldn't get him out. Of course Donagh and Maura couldn't sleep with the boy under the bed, but there he stayed through the long night and into the following day. They again tried to get the child to eat a morsel of food or take a sip of water, but it was no use.

"There's nothing to do but call on Father William," said Maura. "He'll be able to help."

And so Donagh went into the village to talk to the priest about all that had happened. Father William considered a moment, and said: "You must show him some trinket of the sea—a shell or a starfish—and that will entice him out from under the bed. Then take him out on the waters with you tomorrow, as close as you can to the spot where you found him, and toss him back into the sea again."

"But, Father," protested Donagh. "I found him. I should get to keep him."

"Like belongs with like," the priest said sternly. "Return him to the sea." And so the fisherman took the sea child in the boat the next day and rowed toward the spot where he had caught him. All at once the boy let out a laugh of pure delight. He ran past Donagh with nary a glance and jumped, head first, into the waves. Down, down, down he dived, like a great sea bird, and was seen no more.

In the whole time he had been with the O'Donovans, he never said a word.

# The Water Nymphs

THE PEOPLE OF TRALEE were all dancing merrily on the green to celebrate the coming of spring, when there suddenly stepped into the firelight three beautiful young maidens clad in flowing white gowns, with water lilies and roses entwined in their hair. "May we join your Beltaine celebration?" asked one of the maidens, her voice bright and merry as a songbird in May. Although the village women looked upon the three beauties with envy and suspicion, what man could possibly resist them? Three handsome young lads stepped forward, and swung the maidens into the dance.

When the time approached near midnight, and silvery moonbeams flooded the landscape, the maidens said it was time for them to leave. "We can find our own way home," they said politely. "There's no need for anyone to bother." But the three enamored youths followed them as closely as they dared, hoping to discover where the maidens lived.

Imagine the lads' surprise, however, when they saw the girls dance merrily down to the shore of the sea itself and trip lightly from one silvery-tipped wave to another. When they were several yards out, the maidens suddenly paused, and holding out their pale white arms, called to the boys to follow. "We see you hiding in the shadows," they laughed. "Come join us!"

Bewitched by their moon-soaked beauty, the three youths, forgetful of any danger, blindly rushed forward. But instead of embracing the beautiful girls, who suddenly disappeared, they sank down into the moonlit sea forever. At the first stroke of midnight, three crimson, bloodlike streaks were said to stretch from the shore out

to sea. The people of Tralee claim that, years after the boys' disappearance, the same blood-red streaks would appear on the water's surface each May Eve. After showing vividly for a short time, they always vanished as suddenly and mysteriously as they had come. The maidens, it is believed, were not maidens at all, but the dark Fomorian race in disguise.

# The River Sprite

O N THE LEFT BANK of the Shannon, almost smothered by the cool shade of apple trees, is the little village of Kilrush, celebrated because it is one of the favorite haunts of the Fomorian maidens, nymphs as beautiful as they are deadly. Many stories are told about them, and the villagers declare that they can often be seen at a distance.

Two young traders once started out from Kilrush at dawn, and, paddling their curragh, proceeded to head down the river. While one diligently plied the oars, the other gazed down into the water and suddenly shouted, "Regan! Regan! I see her!"

"See who, you idiot?" the other asked, never missing a stroke of the paddle.

"The maiden! Quick, give me your gun!"

"I'm not giving you anything, Martin. You fool! You'll shoot your own foot, so you will!"

But the other ignored his friend's jibes and, seizing the gun, aimed at the water sprite and pulled the trigger. The maiden quickly disappeared from view.

"Do you think I got her?" Martin asked breathlessly.

"You're lucky you didn't shoot a hole in the bottom of the boat," Regan complained. "Now row!"

A strange look suddenly came into Martin's eyes, and Regan knew that he had to row faster. "The sooner we get to the village, the better," he muttered.

"Do you see her, Regan?" Martin smiled. "She's in that river still, beckoning me. Did you ever see such a pretty face?"

"Just row, man, and pay her no mind."

Without any warning, Martin leaped over the side and was quickly carried away by the current.

Three days later his body was washed up near where the Shannon flows into the sea. The people gathered around Regan and heard the strange tale. They noticed, too, that the dead man still clasped the gun close to his breast. Yet, strange to say, a beautiful smile hovered over his rigid blue lips.

Evidently, the people thought, the beautiful demon of the water had forgiven him for his attempt to harm her.

# The Lowland One Hundred

———◆•◆•◆———

R HYS WAS BOTH a drunkard and a fool. Worse, he was the man entrusted with the sea guard defenses of Cantref y Gwaelod, and the lives of hundreds of men, women, and children were his responsibility. He did not take his job seriously, and he would spend many a night drinking hard cider at the Boar's Head Tavern and many a day sleeping off the drink.

One day Prince Elphin came down to inspect the walls

of the sea defense at Cantref y Gwaelod, the Lowland Hundred, for he had heard they were in a dangerous, decayed state. His blood boiled in anger when he saw the ill-kept stone walls. "Bring this man Rhys to me," he hissed through clenched teeth. "I have a wish to speak with him."

"You wanted to see me?" Rhys demanded when he was hustled into Elphin's presence. "Your men dragged me away from my stool, and a full pint measure still on the table before me!"

"I don't give a hang about your drink!" growled Elphin. "I wish to speak to you of your duties. The condition of the sea wall is dreadful! Parts of it are about to give way to the water!"

"Why!" Rhys grinned. "That's the beauty of it! Some parts are sound, and some parts are rotten near through."

"What!" Prince Elphin's eyebrows shot up in surprise. "You admit you've been neglecting your job?"

"I've neglected nothing!" snapped Rhys, now irritated at the proceedings. "And you, your highness, have no respect for antiques! The parts of the wall that are rotten give *elasticity* to the parts that are solid. If it were all solid, it would break down because it is too rigid."

"Whatever are you blathering on about?" asked Elphin. "That makes no sense."

"The way I see it," Rhys continued, "is this: the wall has stood for centuries, and will stand for centuries more, I'm sure. Leave well enough alone. It was half-rotten when I came to this village, and it's held up all these years."

"I will find someone else to tend your duty when I speak of this to my father," Prince Elphin growled. "But until I do, you will remain at your post. If I find you in the tavern, you will be thrown into a cell and the key tossed into the sea."

Later that night at the Boar's Head, Rhys drank himself into his usual stupor. He forgot to shut the leaky old floodgates before he went to bed, and that night a fierce storm blew in from the sea. Gale-force winds sent great waves roaring and clashing and dashing against the weakened sea defenses. The aging wall withstood all that it could and finally collapsed against the might of the turbulent waves. The sea flooded in, drowning cattle and sheep, dogs and people. King Gwyddno's court at Caer Wydno vanished beneath the waves, as did a dozen other towns and villages along the coast. Some say that only one man escaped the havoc by leaping onto his horse, and running just ahead of the advancing water. Others say that there were more survivors, who struggled to rebuild on the mud and debris of a new shoreline.

Nowadays, when the sea is calm and the waters clear as glass, the walls and buildings of Cantref y Gwaelod are said to be visible, and when the currents flow, the church bells sound ever so faintly.

# The Bay of Fools

---◆•◆•◆---

ONCE UPON A TIME, there were three rather foolish brothers who lived near Strumble Head, in the village of Llanwnwr. Bran, Glyn, and Robyn were their names, and together they did not have the sense to come in when it was raining.

It was in August, at the Lammas fair in Fishguard, that

they purchased a round of cheese. They took turns carrying it back to their farm, and it was Glyn who was unfortunate enough to drop the cheese.

Down, down, down it rolled along the cobbled lane and to the sea. The three foolish brothers chased after it, as quick, but not quicker, than the cheese. "Do not overtake it!" shouted Robyn. "Or else we'll wind up in the water as well!"

And so the brothers ran beside the cheese, or just behind it, but were unable ever to grasp it. The cheese tumbled to the edge of the cliffs, not even pausing for a moment, and plummeted to the waves far below.

"We can still reach it," said Bran.

"How?" asked his brothers.

"Like this. Each of us must hang over the edge of the cliff, and take hold of the ankles of the one above us."

"A marvelous plan!" said Glyn.

"Brilliant!" agreed Robyn.

And so Robyn held tightly to Glyn's ankles, and Glyn to Bran's, and in this manner they were able to reach the surface of the water.

"I can see the cheese!" shouted Glyn. "It's just below the surface! We need only stretch a few more inches and I can reach it!"

"One moment!" cried Bran. "I need a better grip!" So the foolish man let go of the rocks he held, and the three brothers followed the cheese on its journey.

Neither Glyn nor Bran nor Robyn were ever seen again. Yet, as strange as it may seem, the brothers will forever be remembered, for the bay they fell into, near the Welsh village of Llanwnwr, is still known as Pwll Ffyliaid, the Bay of Fools.

# The Goat in the Potato Patch

THERE WAS ONCE a man and a woman who lived on a farm in the far north, and their names were Dermot and Una. The wife had a beautiful garden where she grew all sorts of vegetables. There were tangy green beans, crispy red cabbage, kale, peas, leeks, parsnips, and beets. My! But Una loved her potatoes most of all. She would use them in all of her cooking—in soups, in stews, or just plain boiled. She even made potato pancakes with rowanberry sauce for breakfast because Dermot loved them so much.

Now the farmer owned a billy goat who was always getting into trouble. Diabhal, Dermot called him, the Devil. One day Diabhal chewed his way through Una's fence, and he began to sample a bit of everything.

"Phooey!" He spat out the parsnips.

"Yuck!" He spat out the beets.

"Ick!" He spat out the leeks.

Nor did Diabhal like the peas or the kale, the cabbage or the green beans. But when he came to the potato patch his eyes lit up. He *loved* raw potatoes! He dug up the potatoes, and he munched, and he munched, and he munched on them all.

"*Avock!*" shouted Una when she saw what the goat was doing. "Out! Out! Get out of my garden, you troublemaker!" She waved her apron at the billy goat to scare him off, but he turned his back to her. Dermot ran up and the two of them hollered and shouted, they tugged on his rope, and they pushed him from behind. But they couldn't get him to budge one inch. He stood where he was and continued munching on the raw potatoes.

"What are we to do?" wailed Una. "If we don't stop him soon, we will have no potatoes left!"

"Let's ask the hen to help us," suggested Dermot.

Una turned to her brown-and-white speckled hen. "Please, dear hen, if you can get the goat out of the potato patch I will give you extra grain for supper."

The hen flew at Diabhal, pecking at him with her beak and scratching him with her claws. "Get out of here!" she cackled and crowed. "Get out of the potato patch now!"

"I will not!" said the goat.

"I said, get out!"

"No!" The billy goat turned his back to the hen. "You get out!" He kicked her squarely in her tail feathers and sent her flying into the sky.

And he continued munching on the potatoes.

"Perhaps the cat can help us," Una wondered. She turned to her orange-and-white moggie and said, "Dear cat, if you can get Diabhal out of the potato patch, there will be an extra saucer of milk for you at dinner."

The cat ran toward the goat. He arched his back; he scratched and spit. "Una wants you out of her garden!" he hissed.

"No!" said Diabhal. "These potatoes are good; I will not leave.

"I said, get out!"

"No!" said the billy goat as he turned his back to the cat. "You get out!" He kicked him squarely in the tail and sent him flying into the sky. Then he continued eating the potatoes.

"Oh, dear," said Dermot. "What shall we do?"

"Send in the pig. We will give him extra slop if he can get the goat out of the garden," answered Una.

The pig waddled over to where the goat stood. "What are you doing?" he grunted.

"What does it look like?" the goat rudely replied. "I'm eating potatoes."

"Well," snorted the pig, pushing at the goat with his snout. "You better get out of here. The farmer and his wife are not pleased with you."

"No!" said Diabhal. "You get out!" And before the pig knew what was happening, the goat had kicked him in the behind and sent him flying skyward. Then he continued eating the potatoes.

The same thing happened when the farmer sent in his cow.

And his horse.

And his old hound dog.

The goat even kicked a small flock of sheep into the sky. And each time he went right on munching Una's potatoes. Soon she would have none left.

Just as the farmer and his wife were about to give up all hope, a wee voice spoke up.

"Perhaps I can help!"

"Who said that?" Dermot and his wife looked all around them.

"I'm over here!" the wee voice said again. Sitting on a fence post was a tiny spider. "I'm sure I can get the Devil out of your garden."

The farmer looked doubtfully at the tiny gray spider. "What makes you think you can do something that so many larger and stronger animals could not?"

"Just watch, and you shall see what you shall see."

The spider sent out a fine silken thread, and he floated over to where the goat stood. Diabhal never noticed him.

The spider swiftly crawled up the goat's leg. He was so small that Diabhal did not feel a thing.

The spider walked across the goat's furry back, his

footsteps so light that Diabhal never even knew he was there.

The spider softly crawled to the goat's back end, and he . . . *bit* him in the rump!

Diabhal noticed him now. He let out a great squeal and he... jumped high into the sky!

You can be sure that Diabhal never, never went near that potato patch again.

# The Final Hunt

B ROTHER DANDO WAS a good man—kind, well-meaning, and generally liked by all the people of Liskeard. But he was not always able to give them the spiritual guidance that they needed. He was quite fond of the good things in life, such as a comfortable bed, rich food, and strong ale. This in itself was no great sin, for many a Cornishman enjoyed the same. But what kept Brother Dando away from his duties was his love of the hunt.

Whatever the weather, whatever the day, be it Sundays, or saints' days, or feasts of the church, Brother Dando would saddle up his horse and gather his dogs for the hunt. Sometimes he went alone, but if he was in the mood he would bring others with him, men not of the church. Rabbits were his favorite quarry, for they were plentiful and tasty. Brother Dando well enjoyed a hearty rabbit stew.

The people of Liskeard would often shake their heads at Dando's behavior and share their fears with one another. "Surely the Devil himself will come hunting for

Brother Dando if he keeps this up," they whispered, crossing themselves piously. It did not matter that they all liked Dando; they worried over his safety.

How right they were to do so.

Dando was up at daybreak on a Sunday, and he quickly saddled his horse and called his dogs. "There's a southerly wind on the rise," he cheerfully told them, ruffling the ears of his favorite hound. "The day is right fair for the hunt, and I can already smell that rabbit simmering in my pot."

He kicked his heels into his horse's sides and took off. The noisy group dashed through the village, past the people making their way to church, and crossed the river Tiddy over to Lynher and down to Erth Barton, where he had enjoyed good luck in the past.

Pleased to find his friends there ahead of him, they immediately went about the business of the hunt. Many a hare was caught and hung from the saddlehorns, and many a drink was taken from the leather ale flasks that each man carried.

As the sun sank low in the sky, Brother Dando was disturbed to find that he had not one drop left in his flask. "Who's to help me now?" he cried. "My throat's as dry as straw."

When no one offered him a drop of their own, Dando roared, "The Devil take you all, selfish fiends that you are! I'm so parched that I'd go to hell for a pint if the Devil would promise me a cool one!"

Just then a rider stepped out from the shadows. The stranger was elegantly dressed in black wool riding clothes and a wide-brimmed hat pulled low over his eyes. He reached into his cloak to pull out a sparkling silver flask. "Have some of mine," he said, his voice low and smooth. "I'm sure you'll find it to your liking. I know I do."

"That's kind of you," said Brother Dando, taking hold of the flask. He drank long and deep. "You weren't joking!" he smiled in gratitude. "That is fine liquor, to be sure! I've never tasted its like. I'd give my soul to know where you got it."

"Hmmm," the stranger purred. "I think I'll take your hares as partial payment." Quick as a wink, he snatched Brother Dando's catch and ran off into the deepening shadows.

"The Devil you will!" shouted Dando. "That's my supper you have, and I'm not inclined to be sharing!" He kicked his heels into his horse's sides and gave chase after the stranger.

On they went at breakneck speed until they came to the banks of the Lynher. The stranger, who of course was the Devil himself, leapt far out into the water. Brother Dando and his dogs, their throats raised in full cry, followed. All of them—man, horse, and hounds—disappeared with an almighty splash below the surface. The other hunters reached the bank in time to see a huge cloud of steam rise from the surface. Fun-loving Brother Dando was never seen again.

# THE HOWL OF
# THE BANSHEE

# The O'Flaherty Banshee

THE WEIRD WAILING of the banshee usually takes place a day or two before a death is to occur. But it is not always death that the banshee warns of, but also disaster and despair. A story is told in Kerry of one such banshee, where the low, sad notes were heard shortly before a beautiful young girl of the O'Flaherty family was to be married. Cruelly jilted, poor Kathleen died of a broken heart, and the night before her death the dirge of the banshee was heard once again, loud and clear, outside the window of her mother's cottage.

As a rule, the spirit shrieks alone, but sometimes a number of voices are heard singing in chorus. Some years ago a much loved widow of the O'Flaherty clan was taken ill at the family home near Galway. But since her ailment seemed nothing more serious than a light cold, no uneasiness was felt on her account.

Many of the dear lady's friends came by to tend her chores and to cook her supper. There was much talk and laughter around the warm peat fire, and the widow's spirits were lifted considerably.

But as the sun began to slip behind the green hills of Kerry, a weird, wild music rose on the wind.

"Whatever is that, Alana?" they asked the old woman.

The widow O'Flaherty turned several shades paler. It was then that they recognized the singing for what it was. It was not one but a whole chorus of banshees. In just a few hours the lady's illness developed into pneumonia, and by midnight she quietly slipped away. As the widow breathed her last, the unearthly cries burst forth again in a sweet, sad requiem.

# The Hour of Death

TIS A LEE AND a long while now since this story took place, and all the people who witnessed these events have been in their graves for a thousand years. But the old folk still say that at one time everybody in the world knew the exact moment when they would die.

Fionn Lamhfhada knew that he would die in autumn. It doesn't matter to the telling of this tale if he was afraid to die, 'though, no doubt, it didn't trouble him. He knew he would die and there was little to be done about it.

He planted his crops in the spring, just as he had for many a year, but instead of building a sturdy fence around them, all he did was to plant a hedge of a few rushes and furze bushes to guard his crops. His neighbors scoffed at him, but he only said. "What does it matter? I have only to see my crops through the summer. Someone else will have to harvest them."

It so happened that the good Lord sent an angel down to the Emerald Isle to report back to him on the happenings of the people. The angel was much surprised to find Fionn sitting in front of his cottage, sipping a mug of hard cider, and lazily drawing smoke from his clay pipe.

"What are you doing here?" asked the angel. "Why are you not tending your fields on such a fine summer day? And why haven't you a better fence to protect your crops?"

Fionn withdrew his pipe and leaned forward to look the angel squarely in the eye. "The day is too fine to spend working the soil," he said. "And why should I worry about the crop? After I die, it is another man's job

to fence the land and harvest the grain."

The angel returned to heaven, and told the good Lord all that he had seen and heard, and especially about the arrogance of Fionn Lamhfhada. The Almighty was angered by this news, and he shouted, "From this day on, people will have no foreknowledge of their death. I will not have my people lapse into idlenesses!" But the good Lord must have relented some. For sometimes the people of Ireland are granted the knowledge of their death—when the banshee sends out her chilling wail on the eve of disaster.

# Sally McKinnitt's Coffin

*A March cock, a rooster born from an egg laid on the first Tuesday of March, was thought to protect the house from evil.*

THERE WAS A FARM outside of Carlow town where Sally McKinnitt lived with her husband, Thomas. While Thomas worked in the field, Sally stayed home to mind the children and tend to the cooking and the washing.

One endless summer evening, for which Ireland is well known, Sally looked up to see a coffin descending from the sky. At the same moment her rooster jumped up on the house gable, shook his wings, and crowed loudly. He crowed and he crowed and he crowed, until the coffin disappeared.

For a fortnight this continued, and each evening the rooster would crow until the coffin was banished from sight. Thomas McKinnitt began to hate the rooster, complaining that it disturbed him as he trudged homeward for supper.

Then one evening, when he was just coming into the yard, Thomas grew so annoyed with the crowing rooster that he grabbed a wooden mallet and struck it such a blow to the head that it didn't rise again. It was then that he noticed the coffin descending from the heavens.

"Sally, Sally!" he called to his wife in the house. "Come and see this strange marvel!"

Sally stepped from the doorway, wiping her hands on her apron, and looked in horror at the rooster lying dead at her husband's feet. "What have you done?" she cried. "What have you done to my poor March cock?"

"I killed it," her husband said simply. "My head was like to split from his endless crowing day after day. But what's your worry? We can have him for supper."

"Ten thousand curses on you!" wailed Sally. "You killed the rooster, and you've killed me as well! That's my coffin coming down from the sky!" And with her words, both Sally and Thomas looked up to see the coffin descending from the sky, coming closer and closer to the ground near the doorway where they stood.

# The Phantom Knocking

*The* tolaeth *is a sound heard before a death. Sometimes it is a rapping, like a knock at the door, and other times it is like the tolling of a bell. Some people hear it as a shuffle or a thud, as if someone were pounding nails into a coffin. There are even those who claim to hear a tapping at their window at night, along with the fluttering of wings.*

THERE WAS AN old fisherman who lived with his wife on the shores of St. Bride's Bay. One night they heard sounds coming from the lower level of the house.

"Wife? Do you hear what I hear?" the old man whispered.

The poor woman had her blanket pulled up to her nose in fear, but she managed a shaky reply. "I-t s-sounds as if s-someone were opening the back door. But I know I l-left it l-latched."

Just then they heard sounds of shuffling feet, doors slamming, and voices murmuring. There was a great thud, as if something heavy had been dropped on the floor.

"It's coming from the kitchen," said the fisherman. "What should we do?"

"Don't move." His wife clutched his arm. "There's only one thing it could be."

Both stayed where they were, too frightened to investigate, for they knew it could only be the *tolaeth*.

"But which of us is doomed?" the old man whispered.

"Which one of us will die?" asked his wife.

The next night their eldest son drowned when his boat went down during a storm at sea. Several of the villagers carried his body up to his parents' house. As the couple listened and watched in horror, the sounds were the same as they heard the night before: the opening and the slamming of the door, the shuffling of feet, the scraping of chairs, and the thud as the coffin was set on the kitchen floor.

# The Ghostly Funeral

IN THE SOUTH OF Pembrokeshire a man named Defi went to the home of the local vicar. "A strange thing it was that I saw last night," he said when he found the vicar in his summer garden.

"Oh?" inquired the vicar politely. He pulled a handkerchief from his pocket and mopped his brow. "And what might that be?"

"A funeral procession."

"That is indeed strange," said the vicar, "for I did not attend any funeral last night."

"Just the same, I saw all of my neighbors there. Glynn Jones, the widow Bladdud, the Mathry brothers—all of them were there."

"I think you were dreaming, Defi, for there was no funeral last night."

"And the strangest thing of all," Defi continued, as if he had not been interrupted, "was that they carried the coffin up and over the bank instead of taking the road. When I walked around to the gate, I couldn't see them anymore."

"Well, then," said the vicar. "There's an easy enough way to end this nonsense. Show me the spot where you saw the funeral pass. If there was a funeral, the hedge will be trampled down."

Defi returned with the vicar to a spot just outside of his farm. But when they looked, there were no signs of any passage through the hedge.

"I know I wasn't dreaming!" insisted Defi. "Perhaps" —he looked around fearfully—"perhaps it was a phantom funeral, a death portent!"

"There's no such thing as the *toili*," snapped the vicar.

"But…"

"But nothing. We'll speak no more of this," said the vicar sternly. "And I expect to see you in church tomorrow, Defi."

"Please, sir…"

"No more. I'm going back to tend my roses now."

Later that winter, Defi caught a chill and coughed his spirit away. The snows were deep, and as the lane to his house had not been plowed, the coffin was taken up and over the hedge on the way to the cemetery. The good vicar remembered the conversation the summer before, and he shook in fear through the funeral prayers.

# The Corpse Candle

*It is said that St. David, the patron saint of Wales, prayed that the people should have a sign to prepare themselves for death. In a dream he was told that the people would be granted a vision of the* canwyll gorff, *the corpse candle, when death approached. The canwyll gorff might take on the form of a falling light, a light passing along the route of a funeral, or a light hovering in one spot where an accident or death might occur.*

ONE NIGHT THE young schoolteacher Miss Griffiths was staying at the farmhouse of friends just outside Tenby. She could not sleep and lay awake in utter darkness, for the sky was overcast and there was no moon.

She noticed a small light, rather like a tiny star or candle flame, appear somewhere near the door. It moved toward her and stopped just above her feet.

"Jenny, is that you?" she called out.

No one answered.

She was terrified, and when she realized nobody was in the room with her, she screamed loud enough to wake the entire household. The tiny light flickered once and was gone.

Her friend Jenny rushed into the room, Jenny's husband close behind. "What is it, love? Hush, now, Martha, there's a girl. It was only a dream."

"It wasn't a dream, Jenny. I saw it, the *canwyll gorff.*"

The couple exchanged worried glances. "There's no such thing as corpse candles," the husband said firmly. "That's just an old nursemaid's tale."

"I tell you, something's wrong—terribly wrong," the poor schoolteacher wailed. "I think I am dying."

Finally her friends were able to calm her down. She would not remain in the same room, however, and bedded down in a different chamber. Eventually she fell asleep and the incident was forgotten.

A week later, the young teacher went on holiday. While she was gone, her friend Jenny, who had been a healthy, strong woman, fell mysteriously ill. Although the doctor said she would recover, she died within a matter of days. Young Martha was called back for the funeral. When she arrived she was taken upstairs, where she found the body had been laid out in the spare bedroom she herself had occupied—and where the light had appeared.

# WATER BEASTS, WORMS & CREATURES OF THE SUPERNATURAL

# Honey Mead

IT IS WELL KNOWN in every town and village of Ireland that when mead has been kept in a barrel for twenty years without being opened, a dragon will grow in there. Woe to the person who then opens the cask!

In the town of Dalkey, which was once known for the quality and diversity of its mead, a barrel lay forgotten in the cellar of Jared McKee, hidden behind several crates of Spanish wine. Because the barrel lay undisturbed for nearly two decades, a dragon was born there.

First it drank the mead until there was no more left. Hungry, it began to growl from within the wooden barrel, and the noise grew louder and louder until the McKee family could hear it from upstairs. Jared's oldest son, Liam, located the barrel, but none was brave enough to investigate the cause of the growling.

A wise woman lived among the people of Dalkey, and when she got word of the mysterious barrel, she knew what was wrong. "You must bury the barrel deep in the ground; otherwise, the day will come when the dragon will break loose from its prison, and such a monster no one can overcome."

The villagers did as she advised, and since that time nothing has been heard of the Dalkey Dragon. The people of Dalkey, however, will tell you that when the earth shakes and trembles, it is because the dragon is trying to break loose.

# The Black Snake of Inishmore

ONCE UPON A TIME, long and long ago, before St. Patrick came to Ireland, a giant black snake inhabited the waters along the jagged coast of Inishmore. Sometimes, on the rare sunny day, the serpent could be seen basking on the rocks below the cliffs. More often than not he had his treasure with him—goblets of the purest silver, brightly colored jewels, and gold coins that twinkled and flashed like the morning sun upon the waves. Many people walked to the coast to see the awesome sight, but nobody dared to steal the treasure or disturb the slumbering beast.

One day a fisherman came upon the black serpent and his treasure while fishing for halibut. Mahon O'Conghaile his name was, and he was known among those who earn their living from the sea as a brave and daring man. He would take his coracle out on the storm-tossed waters when others would not and laugh as the wind tore at his hair and the rain beat against his fragile boat. O'Conghaile was brave, the Aran Islanders believed, but he was also very foolish.

Because the great serpent was sleeping, Mahon thought that he could row up close and steal a bit of treasure for himself. He dropped anchor and scrambled up the rocks, moving cautiously so that he would not wake the beast.

The fisherman began to fill his coat pockets with diamonds and rubies. With this new wealth, he would never have to work again! Yet when his pockets were full, the man found he was not satisfied. He wanted more. So he took off his coat, laid it on the rocks, and began to pile gold coins on top of it.

In his greed, he forgot all about the snake, and suddenly he was terrified out of his wits by a frightening hissing roar. It reverberated off the rocks and sent shivers down his spine. Dropping his coat, he leaped over the snake's tail and into the water, not caring if he got his socks wet or not, and he felt the serpent's fiery breath lick at the cables of his sweater as he dove beneath the waves.

Mahon swam to his boat, not daring to look back, but the snake did not follow. When he had hoisted anchor and paddled far enough away, he looked back at the serpent, catching a last glimpse as it slid into the water with its treasure, never to be seen again.

# The Piper & the Pooka of November

LONG AGO, A HALF-FOOL lived in Dunmore, in County Galway. Although he was excessively fond of music, he was unable to learn more than one tune, and that was "The Black Rogue." He used to get a good deal of money from the gentlemen, however, for they would get great sport out of him.

One night the piper, whose name was Liam, was coming home from a dance where there had been much laughter and music, and he was half-drunk on *poitín*. When he came to a little bridge that was up by his mother's house, he squeezed the pipes on and began playing "The Black Rogue." A pooka came behind him, and flung the piper up on its own back. Despite the fact that the pooka resembled a horse, long horns grew on either side of its head. Liam got a good grip on them and shouted, "Destruction on you, you nasty beast, let me go home! I have a ten-penny piece in my pocket for my mother, and she wants snuff."

"Never mind your mother," said the pooka. "Never mind your snuff. But do remember to keep your hold. If you fall, you will break your neck and your pipes, and then where will you be?"

They traveled in silence a way, and then the pooka said to the piper, "Play for me 'The Raggle Taggle Gypsy.'"

"I don't know it," said Liam.

"Never mind whether you do or you don't," said the pooka. "Play up and I'll lend you the skills."

Liam put wind in his bag, and he played such music as made himself wonder. "Upon my word, pooka, you're a fine music maker," he said. "But if you don't mind the asking, where is it you're taking me?"

"There's a great feast in the house of the banshee on the top of Crough Patrick tonight," said the pooka. "I'm bringing you there to play music, and, take my word, you'll get the price of your trouble."

"By my soul, you'll save me a journey, then," laughed Liam. "For Father William assigned me a penance to that holy mountain, because I stole the white gander from him last Martinmas."

The pooka rushed him across hills and bogs and rough places, till he brought him to the top of Crough Patrick. Then the pooka struck three blows with his foot, and a great door opened, and they passed through together into a fine room.

The piper saw a golden table in the middle of the room and hundreds of old women, *cailleachas*, sitting 'round it. One old woman, the oldest and ugliest of them all, rose up and said, "A hundred thousand welcomes to you, Pooka of November. Who is this you have with you?"

"The best piper in Ireland," boasted the pooka.

"Is it now?" she laughed. She struck a blow to the ground with her staff and a door opened in the side of the wall, and what should Liam see coming out but the white gander which he had stolen from Father William.

"By my conscience, then," said the piper, "myself and me mother ate every taste of that gander, except for one wing, and I gave that to Red Mary the Witch. And it's she who told the priest I stole his gander! What marvel is this?"

After the gander cleaned the dinner table and carried it away, the pooka said, "Play up—music for these ladies."

The piper played up, and the old women began dancing. They were dancing and dancing and dancing, until they were tired. Then the pooka said to pay the piper, and every woman drew out a gold piece and gave it to him.

"By God's teeth," said Liam, "I'm as rich as the son of a lord!"

"Come with me," said the pooka, "and I'll take you home."

They went out then, and just as Liam was going to ride on the pooka, the gander came up to him and gave him a new set of pipes.

"I'm glad to see there's no hard feelings," said Liam, "seeing as I ate you for supper and all."

The pooka was not long until he brought the piper to Dunmore. He threw the piper off at the little bridge and told him to go home. He said to him, "You have two things now that you never had before, *ciall agus ceól—*sense and music."

Liam went home, a bit dazed and bedazzled, and he knocked at his mother's door, saying, "Mum! Let me in. I'm as rich as a lord and I'm the best piper in Ireland!"

"Hush, now, my son, it's in your cups you are," said his mother.

"No, indeed," said the piper, "I haven't drunk a drop."

The mother let him in, and he gave her the gold pieces, and "Wait now," said he, "till you hear the music I play."

He buckled on the pipes, but, instead of music, there came a sound as if all the geese in Ireland were screeching together. He wakened the neighbors, and they were all mocking him. But when he put on the old pipes, he played melodious music for them. After that he told them all that had happened that night.

The next morning, when his mother went to look at the gold pieces, there was nothing left but dry and crumbling leaves. "Nothing but the gold leaves of autumn," she sighed, "nothing but a faerie trick."

The piper went to the priest and told him the story, but the priest would not believe a word from him. Then the screeching of the ganders and geese began.

"Leave my sight, you thief!" shouted the priest.

But nothing would do the piper till he put the old pipes on to show the priest that his story was true.

He buckled on the old pipes, and he played melodious music. And from that day till the day of his death, there was never a piper in the west counties as good as he was.

# The Basket of Eggs

THERE WAS A GIRL one time, named Berneen Ahearne, who was on her way to Leister to sell her basket of eggs.

"If the price of eggs be up," she mused, "I'll be earning a handful of coins, I will. Yet if the price be down, why, I'll not do too poorly there either, for I have food for a week."

And with those words she saw a wee man sitting down by the hedge, working away at a tiny leather brogue. "Why," she thought, "me luck is getting better all the time. If I had ahold of that wee lad, I'd make him tell me where his treasure is, for the like of such a creatures knows where does gold be hid. I'll be the richest woman in all the village and have servants to sell my eggs."

And so Berneen crept up behind the tiny shoemaker, like a cat would stalk a sparrow, and with a shout caught him around his neck.

Well, the leprechaun let out a howl to be sure, for he was terribly surprised. In all his hundred years he had never been caught so. It was downright humiliating.

"I have you now, my dear own!" crowed Berneen.

"Oh, surely you have, my lady, indeed, yes, you do," the leprechaun tried to smile. "The strength of your thumb is crushing my windpipe, to be sure."

"Never mind that," said Berneen, giving the little fellow a shake. "Show me your treasure!"

"I'd have you to know," he said, his face turning quite purple, "that the pot of gold I could give you is guarded by a fierce serpent."

"What care have I for the creeping beasts of the world?" said Berneen. "A serpent couldn't scare me at all. Besides," she added, her eyes narrowing dangerously, "you know as well as meself that there are no snakes in Ireland."

"Why, you're a brave girl," said the leprechaun. "A clever and wise and handsome one, too, might I add. I've travelled quite far, if truth be told, and I've never seen one to your equal."

"Go on with your prattle," said Berneen, pleased all the same.

"I'm not as young as I used to be," said the leprechaun, "and I couldn't keep up with such a comely lass as yourself. But it's light in the body I am, and I could perch on your basket handle, and you can carry me to the gold, if you don't mind. I'll show you the way."

Berneen paused to consider this but a moment and said, "All right, I'll carry you. But mind now, I'll put you down to walk by my side if I find you are lying."

The leprechaun had not lied, and she didn't feel the burden of carrying him at all. But Berneen was no fool either, and she kept a tight hold of the little shoemaker's ear.

Yet what did the wee lad do but reach down into the basket and begin to toss out the eggs! She twisted his ear painfully, but the harder she beat him the faster he tossed out the eggs! "Ow! Ow! Why are you beating me, Berneen of the flaming hair? I'd have you know when I spill an egg on the ground a full-grown chicken leaps out!"

"Flattery will get you nowhere," fumed Berneen. "So quit your silver-tongued ways!"

"If you doubt me," cried the leprechaun, "turn around and have a look at the chickens that are flocking behind."

With that Berneen turned, mouth agape, and the leprechaun slipped from her grasp. He made one spring from the basket and leaped over a stone wall, vanishing quickly away.

"That tricky creature had me fooled entirely," Berneen shook her head. "And my beautiful eggs, all destroyed! Still and all," she considered, "I can't see it clear to be mad at him. I *am* the finest woman he's seen, and that is a good thing to know!"

# MIRACLES, CHURCHES & HOLY WELLS

# Golden Hood

THERE WAS ONCE a little girl with blue eyes and ebony curls and a tiny dimple on her cheek. Her name was Lorna, and she always wore a wonderful wool cloak with a hood, all gold and fire-colored. The cloak was given to her by her grandmother, whom she loved very dearly, and who was so old that nobody knew her true age. "This cloak will always bring you good luck, Lorna, my love," her grandmother would say. "It was made from a ray of Midsummer sunshine, the most magical beams of all." And as the kindly old woman was considered something of a witch, everyone in the village knew the little cloak was enchanted.

One day Lorna's mother said, "Well, my darling one, I think you are now old enough to walk to your grandmother's cottage alone. You shall take this soda bread and buttermilk to her, along with a good piece of simnel cake for her Sunday treat. Mind your manners, and remember to ask her how she is doing. Say 'please' and 'thank you' if she offers you tea and faerie cakes. Then you are to come back immediately, and do not stop and chatter with people you don't know. Do you understand my meaning well enough, *arwn?*"

"Yes, Mum, I understand," replied Lorna. And off she went with the Sunday cake, quite proud of the fact that her mother allowed her to go all alone.

But the grandmother lived in Duncannon, and there was a big patch of forest for Lorna to cross before she could get to the other village. The path twisted and turned through the wood, and Lorna whistled and skipped along it. Suddenly, she heard a twig snap and stopped in her tracks. "Who's there?" she called out,

more from curiosity than fear.

"A wolf," said a voice as smooth as black silk. From the shadows stepped a great black wolf, the biggest one Lorna had ever seen. He saw that the girl had entered the forest alone, and he was waiting to gobble her up. Little girls were his favorite dish, served best with colcannon and washed down with heather ale. But just as the wolf was about to spring upon little Lorna, some farmers came down the path from the opposite direction, arguing over the price paid for a cow at market. The wolf quickly changed his plan. Instead of pouncing upon Lorna he came trotting up to her like a faithful setter.

"'Tis you, my dear little Lorna," he said with a toothy grin, his tongue lolling out to one side. So the little girl stopped to talk, not knowing that it was dangerous to hear a wolf speak. And she was puzzled, too, how the wolf knew her.

"You know my name, then!" she beamed, her smile as bright as the sun itself. "What is *your* name? Have we met?"

"My name is...um...Wolf. Where are you going, my pretty one, with your basket under your arm?"

"I am going to my grandmother's to take her soda bread and buttermilk, and a good piece of simnel cake for her Sunday treat."

"Ah, I see," the wolf said craftily. "How marvelous! What a splendid and thoughtful child you are. But where does she live, this grandmother of yours?"

"She lives at the other side of the wood in the first house in the village of Duncannon, the little white one with the green shutters in front and the herb garden in back. It's near the windmill, you know."

"Ah! Yes! I know the very one," said the wolf. "As it happens, that's just where I'm going, too. To the village,

I mean. As I have four legs and you have only two, I shall get there before you, no doubt. I'll tell your grandmother that you're coming to see her."

"Why, thank you!" smiled Lorna. "That's very kind of you!"

The wolf began to run as fast as he could, taking the nearest way through the trees, and the little girl went the farthest way about, stopping now and then to gather clover, run after butterflies, or make nosegays of the tiny white shamrock flowers. The wolf was not long in getting to the grandmother's house.

He knocked on the door. Toc! Toc! Toc!

No answer.

He knocked louder. TOC! TOC! TOC!

Nobody.

Then he stood up on his hind legs, put his two forepaws on the latch, and opened the door.

Not a soul was in the house.

The grandmother had risen before dawn to sell herbs in the town. She had left in such a hurry that the bed was unmade, and her great nightcap was sitting atop her pillow.

"Good!" said the wolf to himself. "I've just come up with the most delightful plan!" He had thought to gobble up the old woman first, but seeing that she wasn't there, he decided to have a bit of fun instead.

He shut the door to the cottage and pulled the grandmother's nightcap down over his eyes. Then he lay down all his length on the bed and pulled the bedclothes up to his chin.

All this time Lorna dallied along the path, as little girls do, amusing herself by watching the birds build their nests and the squirrels gather acorns. At last she arrived at the door of her grandmother's cottage. Toc! Toc!

Toc! she rapped on the door.

"Who is there?" said the wolf, softening his voice as best he could.

"It's me, Grandma, your own dear little Lorna. Mother sent with me a big piece of simnel cake for your Sunday treat."

"Ah, my dear! Press your finger on the latch and then push the door. It should open easily enough."

"Why, it sounds as if you have a cold, Grandma," said Lorna when she came in. "Your voice is all harsh and scratchy."

"Ahem, humph," the wolf pretended to cough. "J-j-just a little one, my dear, it's nothing to worry about. Now shut the door, like a good little angel, and put your basket on the table. Then take off your cloak and come sit down beside me. You should rest after your long walk."

The little girl sat down in the chair but she kept her little golden hood on. She leaned toward the bed and was amazed to see how big her grandmother looked in her pajamas. "Oh!" cried she, "you look like my friend Wolf, Grandmother. I never noticed it before."

"That's on account of my nightcap, child," replied the wolf.

"Oh! What a big tongue you've got, Grandmother!"

"All the better for answering, child. Now come closer so Grandma can give you a kiss."

Lorna stood and took a tiny step forward. "And Grandma, what big arms you have!"

"Why, all the better to hug you with! Now come closer, child."

Lorna inched closer. "Grandma, what great ears you have!"

"All the better to hear you with, Lorna. But I am old,

and they are not as good as they used to be. So come closer."

Lorna took another tiny step forward. "Oh! What a mouthful of great white teeth you have, Grandma!"

"All the better for crunching little children with!" the wolf shouted, opening his jaws wide to swallow Lorna.

The girl ducked her head, crying, "*Máither! Máither!*" and the wolf only caught her little hood in his teeth.

Thereupon, oh dear! oh dear! the wolf pulled back, howling and shaking his head as if he had just swallowed red-hot coals!

It was the gold and fire-colored hood that had burnt his tongue right on down his throat, the hood the grandmother said was woven from a midsummer sunbeam. The little hood really was magic and could make the wearer invulnerable!

The wolf, blinded by tears and his throat all scorched up, jumped off the bed and tried to find the door, howling and howling as if all the dogs in the country were at his heels.

Just at that moment the grandmother arrived, returning from town with her long herb sack empty on her shoulder.

"Ah, brigand!" she cried, "wait a bit!" Quickly she stepped aside, and the hurt and maddened wolf sprung through the open doorway. He ran to the stream and drank deeply of the water, trying to quench the burning in this throat.

"You scoundrel!" shouted the grandmother, following him to the water's edge. "You thought you would crunch my little granddaughter. Well, I'll show you, so I will!" With that she pushed the wolf into the stream, giving him quite a soaking.

The grandmother then went inside and helped Lorna dress. The poor girl was trembling and crying. "Well, now," she clucked like a mother hen, "without my little golden hood where would you be now, my darling? In the belly of the wolf, no doubt." And, to restore heart and legs to the child, she made her eat a good piece of simnel cake and drink a good draught of tea, after which she took her by the hand and led her back to her own house. And Lorna promised over and over that she would never again stop and listen to a wolf, so that at last her grandmother hugged her and forgave her.

And Lorna kept her word, and never again did she talk to wolves. Later, her grandmother's magic transformed her into a delicate yellow flower, a boulian. In fine weather she may still be seen in the fields with her pretty little hood, the color of the yellow and orange midsummer sun. But to see her you must rise early.

# The Lovers' Well

O N THE OUTSKIRTS OF Shanmullagh there once stood a prosperous old farm with an ancient stone well in the back. Many people believed that faeries lived in the bottom of the well. Others insisted that it was blessed by St. Patrick himself. But no one knew for sure. The well was there long before any villager could remember, and the waters within were magical indeed.

The village maidens believed that the Korrigans, faeries who lived in the well, had the power to grant wishes. If you made these faeries happy, they would ensure that you were rewarded with a handsome husband and healthy children.

Emer was one such girl. She was desperately in love with a youthful lad named Garrett who lived on the next farm. Garrett was a dashing fellow with warm brown eyes and a dimpled smile.

One fine June morning as Garrett was riding home from the village, he saw Emer drawing water from the well. As the day was hot and he thirsty, he stopped for a drink.

"Emer," he called. "Can you spare me a cup of the water?"

She glanced up at him through thick-fringed lashes and said simply, "Of course."

Garrett stepped down from his horse and stood beside Emer at the well. They both peered down into the dark water far below. The well had a canopy made of strong rowan wood, with a long rope that supported a wooden pail.

"Do you want me to draw the water?" asked Garrett.

"No," Emer shook her head. "I'll get it." Then she pointed down into the well and asked, "Can you see our images?" Their faces were reflected on the cool, calm water below, as clear as any mirror.

Emer reached into her pocket and drew out a shiny new copper. Without another word she tossed it into the well. It shattered their reflections and then, as sunlight slashed through the water's surface, sank and disappeared. The water became still, and Garrett could see both their images again reflected on the surface.

"Why did you throw money in the well?" he demanded, looking at the girl curiously.

Emer blushed deeply. "The faeries like shiny things," she shrugged. "If they're happy with a gift, they often grant a wish."

"And did you make a wish, pretty Emer?" Garrett

asked, brushing away a strand of hair that had tumbled loose from her ribbon.

"I did." She blushed again. At that moment Garrett knew that he was in love with his childhood friend. They both drank deeply from the cup, and walked together the rest of the afternoon, strolling hand in hand and eating ripe gooseberries warmed by the sun. It was not long before the two were married, and they lived, of course, happily ever after.

# The Green Rushes

WHEN ST. PATRICK was traveling through Ulster, he stopped at the cottage of Brendan and Emma O'Madden. The couple was very poor, but they listened to St. Patrick's message and agreed to be baptized.

As the sun sank in the west, the husband admitted, "It's most grievous I am to tell you this, but we have neither candle, nor turf, nor sticks, nor rush light for a fire."

"We usually go to bed with the sun," added his wife, "and awaken with the dawn."

"Are there any green rushes growing in the bog?" asked St. Patrick.

"Aye, there are, surely," said Brendan, "but green rushes won't do us any good."

The saint sent the couple out to gather a bundle of rushes, and he blessed them, and set fire to them, and they gave out a rosy light the whole night long.

# The Church Pillar

PADDY MULLIGAN WOKE with a start to see the kindly monk looking at him with concern. "You've fallen asleep again, Paddy," he laughed.

"Oh, Brother Michael," said Paddy. "You must give me this stone! I'll give you a gold coin in exchange."

"Stone, what stone?" asked the puzzled monk, looking all around.

"The stone from this pillar, of course. A demon of sleeplessness has been haunting my pillow night after night. This is the only place I can rest. As soon as the opening service has ended, I lean my head back against the stone—so that I can direct all my attention to the sermon, of course!—and my eyelids droop over my eyes, my tired limbs relax, and I fall asleep. Some magic power must be inside this pillar. Please let me buy it from you!"

The simple-minded monk excused himself and hurried over to his superior. The abbot listened to the whole story with a twinkle lighting his eye, and finally said, "Brother Michael, go and tell Paddy that our church pillars cannot be removed. But since he has received so much comfort from them, he'd better come in as often as possible to take advantage of the 'stone's' magic powers. The service and the sermon may, in time, actually be heard while he's sleeping."

# A Minor Miracle

THERE WERE ONCE two brothers, Tomas and Wynford Davies, who lived in a village in the north of Wales. One day the elder of the two, Tomas, decided to dedicate his life to his God, and departed for the bleak mountains of Snowdonia. Not once did he look back as he travelled deep into the wilderness. Not once did he try to contact his brother.

It was twenty-five, maybe thirty, years later that Tomas Davies returned to his home. He was as thin as a skeleton, and his skin stretched taut over his sharp features. Yet he smiled when he recognized his brother and called out in a voice rusty from disuse, "Wynford, I have returned."

Wynford squinted at the emaciated vision before him. "My brother, is that really you? Where have you been all these years? You're a sight to make a man weep. But you must have learned something in all that time, or else you would have returned sooner."

"Three decades of living alone, fasting, and praying have given me the power to walk on water," Tomas smiled serenely.

"O my brother," said Wynford, sorrow lodged deep in his heart. "Have you really spent so many years on such foolishness? Why, when I want to cross the river, I only have to hail the ferryman, and I'm there in a matter of minutes."

# FAERIE FORTS, STONE CIRCLES & THE GAP IN TIME

# The Foxhunter's Jig

REMMY CARROL AND Pat Minahan were passing along the soft path at the base of Crockanure one night, when Remmy suddenly stopped. "There's music here," said he.

"Maybe 'tis only a singin' in your head," observed Minahan. "I've known such things, and 'twouldn't be surprising seeing as ye had a drop or two to spare at Murphy's Pub this eve."

"You matched me drink for drink, so you did!" Remmy scoffed. "But hush, I hear it again as distinctly as ever I heard the sound of me own flute. There it is again."

Minahan paused and listened. "Sure enough, ye're right. There's music in the air. Oh, Remmy Carrol, me lad, 'tis lucky you are, for this must be faerie music, and 'tis said that whoever hears it as you did is surely born to good fortune."

"Never mind the luck," said Remmy, laughing. "There's the faerie ring above, and I'll be bound that's the place the music comes from."

"Mayhap it does and mayhap it doesn't," replied Minahan. "There's a difference between hearing the faeries and invading their home. C'mon, Rem, let's just continue on our way. People say there's nothing but trouble to be found within the circle of stones."

"Wives' tales, surely. You've been out of nappies too long to believe in such nonsense, Patrick Minahan. It's embarrassed you should be."

Minahan was not to be brushed off. "'Twas among those stones that Donnal Hennessy had his trial with the faeries, and they turned him to stone, flute and all."

"You don't say?" said Remmy, heading toward the

faerie circle.

"I heard my mother tell it, and she got it from a cousin, who had the story from good authority. Didn't you ever hear of it?"

"I did."

"But you've obviously learned nothing," said Minahan, hurrying to catch up with his friend. "Donnal Hennessy played the flute, rather like yourself, and a mighty fine player entirely. And as he was coming home from a wedding at Rathcormac one fine moonlit night, who should come right upon him on this very same mountain but a whole troop of faeries, singing and skipping and gamboling about. So they up and asked him, as right civil as you please, if he would favor them with a planxty on his flute.

"Now, lettin' alone that Donnal was as courageous as a dog in his own yard and wouldn't even mind facing down the wrath of a woman scorned, he never had the heart to say no when he was asked so nicely—even if it were by a group of faeries. So up he strikes with that fine, lively old tune 'The Foxhunter's Jig,' and sure as I'm telling you, no one could play it better in them days. Why, the very moment the faeries heard it, they all began to caper and dance backwards and forwards, to and fro, like midges of an evening in summer.

"At last Donnal had to stop, and they gathered round him, to find out what was the matter. Your man told them he was dying of thirst, so he was, and that he must have something to wet his whistle.

"'To be sure!' said a spritely young faerie with a toss of her hair. 'That's only reasonable. Bring the gorson a drink of something good!' So she handed Donnal just a faerie-finger full of a drink that had a mighty pleasant smell, and filled a harebell cup of the same for herself. 'Here's to you,' says she. 'There's not a headache in a hogshead of it, and not a gauger's rod has ever come near it, I warrant ye. 'Twas made in Araglin of mountain barley.'

"Well, with that she drank to Donnal, and Donnal raised his little weeny measure to his lips. Though it wasn't more than the size of a thimble, he drank at least half a pint out of it, and yet it was as full as ever it was before.

"Arrah! But that drink did give your man the boldness of a lion, that it did. And nothing would do the fool but challenge the whole lot of them to equal him at playing the flute.

"Some of them who were tenderhearted advised him to keep quiet and not to try. But the more they persuaded, the more he insisted. At long last the faeries' best flute player came forward and took up the challenge.

"So at it they went, did Donnal Hennessy and the faerie musician, playing against each other until the cock in the nearest house crew. And the whole gang vanished into a cave in the hillside and whipped your brave Donnal along with them, flute and all.

"But that's not the end of it all. The faeries had expected to humble the boastful musician, but they could not. He was the equal of, aye, and better than, any musician in their troop. But to punish him for his boldness, they changed your man into a stone statue, which they set in the middle of the faerie ring, where it remains to this day.

"And that's what happened to Donnal Hennessy in the end for offending the good people."

"Hmm, well, a good story to be sure," said Remmy. "But the telling of it has taken half the eve. It'll be cockcrow soon, and we'd best be on our way. Our trip to the stone circle will have to wait another day."

"As you wish, Remmy, as you wish!" laughed Minahan.

# The Queen beneath the Hill

MANY YEARS AGO, long before your grandfather's grandfather walked the earth, there ruled a certain King Fergus the Young. He was well-loved and good to the people, but he eventually turned his subjects against him when he mistreated Aine, the beautiful brown-haired daughter of his vanquished enemy, Oirbsen, King of the Western Ocean. Rather than be forced to marry Fergus, the sea princess Aine took her own life and followed her father to the grave. She was buried in a prominent mound, known throughout Limerick as Knockaney.

It was a great many centuries later when Ruari Dubhlaoch, as fine a fiddler as ever you'd find, was returning home from a wedding party. He was known all through County Limerick, if not the whole west of Ireland, for the skill in his fingers. Faerie-blessed, the people said, and his music was always in high demand. Long after the bride and groom had left the ceildh, the music man kept time with the dancing feet of his guests. He kept them leaping about through the night and right to the dawn of the next day. He was rewarded with a great many tumblers of punch, and not a few cups of poítin were given to him by the bride's parents. In a rare mood, he played lively jigs, reels, hornpipes, and strath-speys one after the other as if a man possessed. What energy! As the sun began to peek over the edge of the horizon to banish the darkness of night, the fiddler bade farewell and began the journey home. He would have made it home all right if he hadn't been so tired. But since he was all worn out from playing, he decided to rest.

Unfortunately for him it was on the enchanted rath of

the tragic sea princess. He laid down his sack and sat down on the cool green grass. The sweet morning air, the soft singing of birds and the sun-kissed sky struck a cord in his heart. Ruari took out his fiddle and struck up a particularly beautiful air to greet the day.

As he played, all fell silent; even the breeze died down as if to pause to listen to his haunting melody.

When the last lingering notes drifted off, a tiny door opened in the side of the rath. A crowd of fierce and scaly demons with leathery wings and sharply pointed teeth flew out and whirled in the air above Ruari's head. Before the poor musician could call out a single "God bless and keep me!" they seized Ruari, his sack, and his fiddle and rushed them into the hill. Thwack! The earth clapped shut behind him.

"What! What are ye doing? Put me down at once, I say!" Ruari howled as he was dragged down a dimly lit passage. "Come now, watch me fiddle!" He was too enraged and worried about his violin to be afraid or wonder where he was being taken.

At the end of the passage was a golden door that seemed to melt away as the crowd rushed through. The fiddler's eyes seemed to nearly pop from his head when he saw the green-lit chamber he was brought to.

Bright and blue-green as seawater, the roof of the Great Hall of the Sidhe arched high overhead. But it did not take away from the light of those within. An assortment of odd faces turned toward Ruari. There were faeries as fine-boned as angels, and others with teeth and claws and large, fur-covered limbs. A gathering of merfolk swam lazily in an underground pool, and leprechauns and roans—doglike creatures with the souls of men—cavorted on the smooth-tiled floor. Ruari was suddenly afraid and chilled, as if he had been plunged into the winter waters of the Liffey.

Hundreds of glowing lamps lit the room, and the entire chamber was supported by intricately carved marble pillars. The oakwood tables were laden with crystal-like fruits and golden, sparkling wine. As Ruari's gaze traveled down the length of the table, past the silent, watchful faces of the host, his eyes locked with those of the Faerie Queen. Ice-blue they were, and they chilled him to the marrow. Her gown was starlight, her hair like the sky before dawn. A crown of white gold sat atop her head, and it was set with moonstones and sapphires. A blue diamond pendant encircled her throat, catching the blue firelight of the lamps. She stood. "Welcome, Ruari," she said in Gaelic. "I am Aine." Those were the only words he understood at the whole banquet. The faeries chattered around him in their own strange, musical language.

For a long time Ruari watched a procession of noble faerie lords and ladies as they presented gifts to Queen Aine. The men bowed very low and the women dipped in curtsies. It was finally Ruari's turn to be formally introduced. But what had he to give? He hesitated, but was prodded along by those who had dragged him in. He stood shaking at the foot of the throne. His clothes were rumpled and plain, and he felt coarse in such a fine company and before such a noble queen. He knew he was unable to imitate the graceful bows of the Queen's attendants. He took his cap in his right hand and ran the other through his hair to straighten it; then he gave a quick bob of his right knee.

Coarse faerie laughter rippled down the length of the table. Ruari blushed and stared at his feet, hurt and embarrassed.

"Sit by me," Aine purred with a smile. She gestured beside her and a bench rose from the ground.

From the bard's place of honor Ruari placed the fiddle under his chin. He watched as the faeries left their spots at the table and stared as it melted into the ground. They were ready to dance and he puzzled for a moment as to what to play for them. A country dance tune? His eyes took on a glimmer of mischief and he played "The Faerie Dance," most appropriate for the occasion.

"Well done," cried Aine when he had finished. "You have brought me a fine music-maker, indeed." She held out her hand and in it appeared a brilliant silver and crystal goblet. It was filled with ruby-red wine, as dark as blood. "Will you share a glass with me, Ruari?" she asked slyly.

Something in Ruari screamed "No!" but he took the cup from the Queen's hand and drank it down. It burned like fire.

"Play, minstrel," the Queen said with a cat's smile on her face, and Ruari was obliged to obey. He remembered, too late, that if a mortal eats or drinks anything in the faerie world, he will be trapped there forever. He played jigs, reels, and country dances until the faerie host had had their fill. They disappeared with a flash. The lights were dimmed and the piper sat in near-darkness. It was gloomy and cold.

"They come and go like the wind," said a voice, a human voice. Ruari looked in the corner where it came from. Unnoticed before, a human girl-child sat huddled in the shadows. "Something captured their interest and they were off to see it. Who knows when they'll return. It could be minutes or days."

"How long have you been here?"

The child cocked an eyebrow at Ruari and sighed. "In our time or theirs?" she sighed. "I am still eight in years, although I suspect that everyone I know is long dead."

She looked at Ruari. "You shouldn't have drunk their wine."

"I know. I forgot."

Bells rang and trumpets sounded, heralding the return of the faerie host, although neither Ruari nor the child could see any of them. The fiddler refused to sit around in idleness, however, and he was determined to find a way out. He took the child by the hand and led her down twisting, dark corridors. Ruari thought they were headed back the same way, and although they spent several hours in weary search, it was to no avail. They could not find the exit. To make matters worse, they could hear the faeries flying overhead, chattering in their strange language. They rested against the walls of the cavern.

"I'm hungry," said the child.

"Hush!" whispered Ruari. "Be very quiet." Above their heads a gathering had formed. In the half-light Ruari could glimpse the faeries mounted on fiery-eyed chargers. Each one was carrying an elegantly carved bow. It was a hunting party!

Gripping a spear tightly in his fist, the red-cloaked leader raised it above his horned head and shouted, "*Liacso sarod!*"

"*Liacso!*" repeated the warriors down the line, each in turn. "*Liacso sarod! Liacso sarod!*"

There was a creak and a groan and the earth parted. Light flooded the passageway and Ruari could glimpse the green rolling hills of Knockaney. He sprang for the doors, but they slammed shut in his face. "*Damnú air!*" he cursed.

"But we know the password now!" the child reminded him.

Ruari spun around. "We do, don't we?"

They stood beside one another and shouted, "*Liacso sarod*!" The earthen door opened as before and Ruari and the child scrambled out. They were standing atop the Mound of Knockaney.

"We're free!" The child wiped away a tear. "We're home."

Ruari adopted the child, whose name was Grainne, for she was correct in the fact that her family had died more than 150 years ago. Cursed faerie time! He himself had only spent a night in the hill, but when he returned to the world of men it was one year later.

For many seasons afterward Ruari played his fiddle at fairs and weddings, christenings and wakes, everywhere his spirited music was needed. And always, always, he told the tale of his night spent in Queen Aine's keep.

# Whiskey on a Sunday

Toíbi and Fergus made the journey to the inn for some whiskey, since New Year's was not far off and the next day was Sunday, when no spirits would be sold in the village. After they paid for their whiskey, they returned with it in jars on their backs, and some of it, you can be sure, in their bellies. On the way home, they saw a brilliant light before them. Shortly after that they heard sweet music and a shout of great rejoicing coming from the place where they saw the light. Ever since they were boys they had been told that this was a faerie rath, but they had never believed it. Now, when they reached the side of the hill, they saw that it was open and that faeries were playing a dance.

Toíbi took out his knife and thrust it into the side post of the door, since metal was a protection against faeries, and he and Fergus made sure to stand on the outward side of the shining blade. However, Fergus did not remain there long; being a musician himself, he could not keep still and sprang into the hill shouting, "Up with it!" And then he began, with the jar on his back, to dance in the circle of faeries.

Toíbi laughed at the antics of his friend, and after a while called out, "Fergus, best come along now, or else we won't make it home in time for New Year's.

"Whisht! We have plenty of time!" said Fergus. "I have not yet danced one reel!"

Then some of the faeries came to the door and tried to coax the other man in. "We're having a grand time," they insisted. But Toíbi made sure to remain where he was. After a while longer he called to Fergus again, "C'mon, man! Let's go! It's almost cockcrow!" But no amount of arguing would do any good at all. He kept getting the same reply: "But I've yet to hear the fiddler strike up a reel!"

Toíbi saw that there was no convincing his friend, and so he drew his knife from the doorpost and stepped back. The faerie knoll closed and he went home.

When he arrived at his own cottage, everyone asked him where he had left Fergus. He told them everything that had happened and how he had left his man dancing in the faerie hill. But there was not one of them that credited the story. Instead, they insisted he must have killed his neighbor and invented the whole tale.

"Sure now, why would I do that?" he cried, but it was in vain that he protested his innocence. They put him under guard and pronounced the death sentence on him. "But it's God's own truth I'm telling you! Only give me a year and a day to clear my name." After much debate, they at last granted him that.

When the next New Year's came around, Toíbi went the way of the faerie knoll in which he had left his friend. The hill was open and Fergus was now playing the fiddle for a dance. Toíbi thrust his dirk into the doorpost and called out, "What are you doing, in God's name?"

"C'mon now, man, they asked me if I'd play them but one tune. I'll only be a moment longer."

"Do you know how long you have been here?"

"No more than five minutes, surely. I can't fathom your concern."

"Five minutes! Try a year and a day! Your family and friends all think you dead and I that killed you. They intend to hang me tomorrow unless I bring you home with me alive and whole."

"Very well," Fergus grumbled. "I'll come as soon as I come to the end of the repetition."

"You've been playing that repetition for a year now, and you're no closer to ending it now than you were then." And with those words Toíbi grabbed his friend and yanked him out of the hill. As soon as he pulled his dirk from the doorpost, the hill closed back up and they could no longer hear the music.

Together they carried Fergus's jar of whiskey back to the village. But the whiskey in the jar was all gone, and in its place was plain rainwater.

# The Minstrel's Question

A**T THE END OF** the potato famine in Ireland, there was a man living in Killarney and his name was Tadhg O'Moriarty. He had made it through those hard times, but afterwards became terribly ill, so ill that the priest needed to be called. As it was Samhain night, Father Donncha O'Reachtaire did not wish to go alone, so he took one of the altar boys with him.

They walked swiftly to the farm at the edge of town, and as they turned down the lane toward the house, they came across a man playing on a harp, his back to them. "Sheoguey creature," the altar boy mumbled, quickly crossing himself. "Who else would be out on Samhain? All decent men are safe in their beds."

"Nonsense!" the priest waved the boy's concerns aside. "It's just one of the villagers, unable to sleep." He fumbled in his pocket for a copper.

"I don't need your money, priest, I have no use for it," the minstrel said before Father Donncha could offer him the shiny coin.

"But I insist," he protested. "It's customary to pay the music maker for his craft."

The moonlight shifted as the man turned to face them, and his features were lost in shadow. "If you wish to help me, priest of the parish, there is something you can do."

"And what may that be?" asked Father Donncha.

"Tadhg O'Moriarty will die this night," the piper said softly, and the altar boy cowered behind the priest.

"What?" Father Donncha chuckled nervously. "How do you know that? You don't have the look of a banshee about you."

"Nevertheless, I tell you he will die."

"Well," the priest said, a little more loudly. "What has this to do with you?"

"As Tadhg breathes his last, ask him where I will go on the Last Day."

"I knew it," jittered the poor altar boy, "Did I not say he was a sheo…"

"Hush!" snapped the priest. But he too was taken a little aback by the minstrel's request. "I will ask him," he promised, "but who shall I say you are?"

"Just say to him, 'The man on the road to Slieve Luchra wishes to know.'"

"That I will do," Donncha nodded. The priest then went to the house of Tadhg O'Moriarty, and after he went inside, he forgot all about the minstrel. The man in bed was deathly pale.

He said the last rites over him and anointed him with oil. Then there was nothing left to do but wait. As he held the hand of the dying man, they could suddenly hear the strains of a lament playing on the wind. The priest remembered the question he was to ask Tadhg. "The man on the road to Slieve Luchra wishes to know where he will go on the Last Day. Do you know?"

The man in the bed smiled weakly. "I do. Of course. Tell him, tell him that if he has enough blood in his body to write his name, then he will return to heaven."

"Return?" the priest asked in confusion. "What do you mean by such a remark as that?" But it was no use. Tadhg was dead.

Father Donncha and the altar boy left the house shortly before dawn, and the minstrel was waiting anxiously for them. "Well?" he asked. "What news?"

"I know not what to make of such an answer, but

O'Moriarty's last words were, 'Tell him if he has enough blood in his body to write his name, then he will return to heaven.'"

"It's blood that he wants, is it?" the man suddenly howled. The altar boy nearly fainted in fright, but the priest stood firm.

"Tadhg is gone, man, he doesn't want any blood."

"No, you foolish man! I don't mean him!" the minstrel whipped a dirk from his sleeve, and Father Donncha stumbled back, afraid of being struck. The harper took the knife and stabbed at his own heart. But not a single drop of blood fell. He stabbed at himself again and again, but there was nothing, just a black bile that gurgled and frothed like the foam on the sea.

The priest crossed himself rapidly. "What are you, man? What do you want?" he asked.

"I was cast out of heaven with the other faeries for my crime of doing nothing while Our Lord was challenged by Lucifer Morningstar. I have never harmed another soul or even wished to! But now that I see I have nothing to gain and nothing to lose, I will do nothing but evil to the race of men from now on. Beware, priest, lest we meet again!" There was a black flash of smoke and fire, and the minstrel was gone. The priest returned to his own home, leading back the blathering altar boy. Luckily, he never encountered the faerie man again; however, he never left his home after dark, either. As to Tadhg O'Moriarty? No one knows why, on his deathbed, he was able to catch a glimpse of Judgment Day.

# The Fair Island

THERE'S A GREEN ISLAND called Tír-nan-Og, the Island of Youth, that lies far out in the western oceans. Age and death have not found it, nor have tears or sorrow ever burdened the heart of one who dwelt there. It is there that the apples of immortality grow, and it is there that the curative elixir that bubbles up from the fountain of youth is found. Most people say only one man has ever gone there and returned, the great bard Ossian, but there have been others.

Tiernan Farrell lived in the Aran Islands, and he was, like most men of the islands, a fisherman by trade. He owned a small curragh which he sailed alone on the open waters each evening, returning by dawn the next day.

One day, as Tiernan was bringing in a haul of gurnard, he saw standing on the dock the biggest man he had ever seen. He was easily two feet taller than Tiernan himself. He had flaming orange hair that stood on his head in all directions, as if he had never seen the likes of a comb, with a beard and mustache to match.

Grabbing hold of the line that the fisherman tossed to him, the giant called in a booming voice, "Tiernan Farrell! They tell me that you have a boat that can carry cargo between islands."

"They told you right," said Tiernan carefully. "But it depends on the cargo."

"Why, you've nothing to worry over. It's just a cargo of meat. I have the directions for you."

"All right," Tiernan agreed, and before long they had loaded the cargo into his boat. Then the giant himself stepped in, causing the boat to ride low in the water.

"Don't worry." The red-haired giant laughed at the

look on Tiernan's face. "We'll make the journey safely enough."

"Surely you have enough meat here to feed a small village," said Tiernan as they pulled away from shore.

"You could say that," laughed the giant again. "Aye, you could indeed."

Tiernan hoisted his sails and they headed out to sea. The giant kept them on course, and they sailed far, perhaps farther, than the fisherman had ever sailed before. "Are you sure you know where we're going?" he asked.

"Of course. We'll reach our destination soon."

But a thick fog crept over the waters, and Tiernan was forced to steer blindly, hoping that his strange passenger knew where he was taking them. From the feel of the ocean and the tug of the wind, he assumed they were still heading west.

On the third day, the fog finally lifted, and Tiernan saw before him a fertile green island sparkling like jewel in the water. He felt the island beckon to him and knew he would find peace there.

"Tír-nan-Og," he sighed. "I thought it was a myth."

"Here we are," said his companion cheerfully.

Tiernan hardly noticed what he was doing as he pulled the boat to shore and secured it well. He stepped lightly onto the beach, and it was as if a terrible load had been taken from his shoulders. "I feel like a youth of twenty again!" he laughed. "I've never felt more alive!"

He spun around to his companion, "Who are you?" he asked.

"One of the island's inhabitants," the man answered. "Help me unload this meat, and then it's time for you to go."

"Go?" Tiernan asked incredulously, running a hand over the smooth skin on his face. "I'm young again. I have no intention of going anywhere."

"Hmmm," the giant said, considering a moment. "Then take a drink with me." He pulled from his bag a huge drinking vessel and poured from a sack a sweet, amber-colored liquid. "Drink up, Tiernan, my lad," he said.

Tiernan grasped the vessel. It was so heavy that he needed two hands to lift it to his lips. When he had finished drinking, he set it down again. Suddenly he felt woozy and needed to lie down. "That was fine mead, indeed, but it has made me tired. I'll just have a bit of a sleep," he mumbled, "and then I'll help you."

"Fair enough," said the red-haired giant. "Pleasant dreams."

When Tiernan awoke, it was night, and he found himself in his curragh floating in the middle of the ocean. Green-gray water stretched in all directions, with nary a bit of land in sight. He reached a shaking hand to his face and felt the familiar wrinkles around his eyes. "I've been cheated," he said, disappointment a bitter ache in his chest. His eyes fell on a large sack at his feet. He opened it, spilling out countless gems and gold coins."

"Well," he mused, smiling down at his treasure. "If I can't have youth, I'll settle for wealth." Glancing up at the stars above him, he steered his way home.

# CURSES &
# INCANTATIONS

# A Tale of Wine & Fishes

A TRAVELER ONCE CAME to Leixlip along the River Liffey, entered the village inn, and called to the host, "Bring me a jug of wine, for I've a powerful thirst about me!" The innkeeper, Myles Keegan, a thrifty man if ever there was one, seized his crock and marched down into the cellar where there were two faucets. He turned the first one very gingerly, indeed, and partly filled the jug with sour wine. Then, rushing to the other faucet, which was set in the wall, he turned it full-cock and allowed the water from the Liffey to flow freely until the jug was quite full.

Myles Keegan then marched upstairs again and filled his guest's tumbler. "Ah, this is a fine vintage, the finest you'll find in all of Ireland. Drink your fill and welcome!"

The guest drank eagerly, but made somewhat of a face when he tasted the sour drink. He slammed the tumbler on the wooden bar top and declared, "It's ashamed you should be to serve a guest such a drink! You've mixed water with your wine, haven't you now?"

"I'm offended that you'd accuse me so!" declared the innkeeper.

"Then pour me another glass!" demanded the patron.

The innkeeper muttered under his breath, and snatched up the crock to pour another tumbler of wine. But as he did so, three little fish passed from the jug into the tumbler, where they merrily swam around and around, convicting the innkeeper for all to see.

"Didn't anyone ever tell you," said the innkeeper's wife with a laugh, "that you're supposed to strain the water first?"

But the traveler was not amused. "A curse upon you then!" he cried. "A curse on all of Ireland. May you never be able to make a proper vintage!"

And that is why, to this very day, Ireland is not known for its wine-making industry.

# The Giants' Pot

THREE GREAT GIANTS once lived in a cave along the rocky northern coast of Donegal. Their appetites were fully as great as their size, and, as they ate nothing but porridge, they asked a neighboring founder to make them the biggest pot ever seen in the five provinces. After cooking their porridge for the first time in this colossal new pot, the giants sat around it, dipping their spoons in unison into the center of the oatmeal, drawing them out very full, opening their mouths, shutting their eyes, and solemnly gulping down each morsel. When the last spoonfuls had thus been disposed of and no porridge remained in the bottom of the vessel, each giant carefully licked his spoon clean, and running it through his belt declared that the pot was just the right size to satisfy his appetite. "And blessed it must be, for never have I tasted better porridge," each told the other.

Time passed on. Although the pot remained unchanged and the giants grew no larger, it seemed as if, little by little, they had less and less to eat. They daily drew their belts tighter to prevent their spoon from falling through. Finally, one of them declared, "Every day my portion grows less. The pot is cursed, surely. I

always knew Padraic Colum was a witch's son!"

His brothers agreed with him, and they angrily invaded the founder's shop. "Remove your curse at once, old man, or you will regret it sorely!"

The poor man was flummoxed by their accusations and vainly tried to defend himself. "Never in me life have I dabbled in the dark arts. How dare you accuse me like this!" But seeing as he was getting nowhere, he finally said, "Bring the pot to me, and I'll see where the fault lies."

The giants immediately went in search of their porridge pot, and tipped it up on one side so the founder could walk in, for it was so large that he could not look over the brim when it stood upright on the floor. The giants watched him walk in, and were greatly surprised to hear him burst into peals of laughter. Then, setting aside their questions, he ran into his shop, came out again with a hoe, and in a very few moments had scraped out a great heap of dried porridge which had gradually formed a thick crust all around the pot's lining.

His work done, he turned to the giants and coolly said. "May I inform you, me good men, that you must *scrape your pot clean*, and you will find that from now on it will always contain the same amount of porridge."

The giants took this advice to heart and taught their descendants, and all the people in Donegal, that one of the most important maxims in life was to "scrape their pots clean."

# Shon ap Nudd

SHON AP NUDD WAS a warrior in the court of Arthur. He longed for adventure. And so, without a word to anyone, he headed into the forest with nothing but his horse, his armor, and his sword. As he passed through a thick strand of rowan trees, he saw something round and pale and gleaming in the shadows. When he took a closer look, he saw that it was a human skull, bleached white by time and weather. He swore that it was grinning at him.

"I wonder what happened to you, poor fellow," Shon mused.

"My big mouth brought me here," the skull replied.

Imagine Shon's astonishment, for never before had he heard the dead speak. "Now this is an adventure, indeed," he finally managed to say. "Wait until I bring you back to the court. Surely the king will let me sit at the high table when I present him with such an object! Surely I will have my choice of maidens!"

He bent down to place the skull in his sack when he heard a rustle behind him. Cursing himself for leaving his sword by his horse, he slowly turned to see who was there. It was a knight in black armor.

"What are you doing here, in these my woods?" the knight demanded angrily. "No one may come here without my leave."

"I was following the path when I happened to see a skull on the side of the road—a talking skull!" Shon hoped that his voice did not tremble.

"A talking skull?" the black knight repeated. "Since I was a babe at my mother's knee I have not heard of such a thing. The dead cannot speak."

"But they can!" Shon gestured at the skull. "And this one just did!"

"Hmmm," said the black knight, glancing down at the grinning white bones. "I demand proof of such a miracle. If you can get this pathetic skull to speak again, I will let you get your sword and we will fight in fair combat."

"And if it will not speak?" Shon asked.

"Then I will strike off your head where you stand, and let your skull join this one in eternal rest," the black knight said grimly.

Shon ap Nudd agreed to the challenge—what else could he do? But he was confident that the skull could speak; he had heard it do just that with his own ears.

"Speak, skull," he addressed the white bones, "speak so that this honorable knight will know I tell the truth."

But the skull was silent.

A nervous flutter gripped his stomach and sweat broke out on his forehead. "Speak!" he demanded.

The skull lay still on the forest floor, staring up at the two men with empty sockets.

"Come on, now!" he begged. "Say just one word! Anything!"

"I grow weary of this," sighed the black knight. "Even though I caught you trespassing on my lands, I was ready to offer you a fair fight. But you dishonor yourself with your lies. You are not worthy of challenging." Before Shon could protest, the black knight cut off his head. It rolled to the ground and came to rest beside the gleaming white skull.

When the knight left, taking Shon's horse and armor with him, the skull grinned at the head beside him and asked, "Well, Shon, what brought you here?"

"My big mouth brought me here," the head sighed.

# WISE WOMEN
# & WITCHES

# The Dream of Owen Mahoney

THERE WAS A MAN long ago living near Mullinahone, in Tipperary, named Owen Mahoney. A tenant farmer of the gentleman of the place, he was himself a prosperous, quiet, contented man. There wasn't a care or concern on Owen, except for one desire, and that was to have a dream, for he had never had one.

"Owen Mahoney!" his wife exclaimed whenever he talked of the matter to her. "Never in my life have I heard a more ridiculous complaint! It's an easy night's rest you have, unburdened by dreams. But if you feel you must dream, talk to the witch woman, and perhaps she can help."

"Perhaps I'll do just that," said Owen.

One day when Owen was digging potatoes for his master, a woman with hair of flame and eyes like bottle glass came out to the field. *"Dia dhuit,* Owen!*"* she called.

Owen peered up at the witch woman and smiled cautiously. "And good morning to you as well, Maude Muldoon.

"I dreamed of you last night, Owen."

"Is that a fact?" he asked, not sure of Maude's meaning.

"'Tis, yes. I dreamed last night that you were given your heart's desire."

"I am quite happy with my life. There is nothing I desire more than a hot meal, a warm fire, a soft bed, and a wife who loves me. All these I have."

"Well," said the wise woman. "In my dream a man told you to put out your fire in the hearth, make your bed in its place, and sleep there the night. Then you too

will have a dream as others do."

"Ah!" said Owen. "Can it be true?"

"This I know not. I only thought I should come and tell you of it." And with that, Maude Muldoon left the fields as silently as she came.

That night, Owen began to draw the fire out of the hearth, and his wife thought that he had lost his senses, so strange were his actions. But when he told Lorna of the witch's dream, she decided to make her bed in the hearth as well. It was not long after Owen was asleep that there came a knock at the door.

"Get up, Owen Mahoney! The master wants you to take a letter to America!"

Owen got up and put his feet into his boots. "It's late you come, messenger." Then he shook his head to remove the cobwebs of sleep. "America, you say?"

The messenger handed him a letter. "America," he repeated.

Without a word to his wife, Owen left the cottage and began to walk the road to Galway, where surely he'd be able to catch a ship to America. As he was passing the foot of Sliabh Charn, he met a red-haired farmhand, and he herding cows.

"*Dia dhuit*, Owen Mahoney!" the man called.

"*Dia is Muire dhuit*," returned Owen. "Everyone knows me, and I don't know anyone at all."

"Where are you going this time of night?" asked the man, and Owen could see that his eyes were as green as the fields in springtime.

"I might ask you the same," replied Owen, "for I find it strange you should be herding cows at midnight. But I'm going to America with a letter from the master. Is this the road to America?"

"It is," the man nodded. "Keep straight west, and you

should reach it by morning. But how will you cross the water?"

"I'll cross that bridge when I come to it," laughed Owen, delighting in his own joke.

He took to the road again, till he came to the shores of the sea. There he saw a crane standing on the shore on one foot. "*Dia dhuit*, Owen Mahoney!" the bird called.

Owen stepped closer and could see that the crane's head was crowned with red feathers, and his eyes were as green as the fishes that swam in the Shannon. "*Dia is Muire dhuit,*" he said. "Everybody knows me, and I don't know anyone."

"What are you doing here?" asked the bird.

"I might ask you the same," said Owen, "for I've never before seen a bird possessing the speech of a man. As for myself, I'm on my way to America to deliver a letter for my master. Only now that I'm here, I don't know how I'll cross. It seems I've left my wallet at home and I haven't a copper to spare to pay for my journey by boat."

"Well, then," the bird peered at him. "Set your two feet on my wings and sit on my back. I'll take you to the other side."

Owen climbed on the back of the crane, and she rose over the sea. But she hadn't flown more than halfway when she cried out, "Owen Mahoney, get off me, for I'm too tired to carry you any longer!"

"What?! May you be seven times worse this day twelve months, you rogue of a crane!" cursed Owen. "I can't get off you now, so don't ask me."

"It's a rude man you are," replied the crane, "and I won't tolerate your company any longer." With a shake of her wings, she tossed Owen on top of a fluffy white cloud, and he watched in dismay as the crane flew off.

To be sure the cloud was as soft as a down quilt, but

he couldn't stay here all night! He had to get to America! Just then he saw a ship passing not far below.

"Help! Oh, help!" Owen cried to the sailor on deck.

The sailor ran a hand through his unruly mass of red hair, and with eyes as green as the depths of the sea he squinted up at the man on the cloud. "*Dia dhuit*, Owen Mahoney. What are you doing up there, boy-o?"

"*Dia is Muire dhuit*. Everyone knows me, and I don't know anyone at all. It doesn't matter how I got here, but will you help me down?"

"That I surely will. You only need jump and you can land on the deck."

"I'm sure to miss the deck, and I'll drown for sure!" wailed Owen.

"No, you will not!" called the sailor. "Fling down one of your boots, and we'll see which way it falls."

And so Owen, his hands gripping tightly to the silver lining of the cloud, dangled over the edge, and kicked off one of his boots.

"Oof, ow, oh! Who's trying to kill me?" came a scream from below.

Owen peered down, and saw his own dear wife, Lorna, glaring up at him.

"I didn't know whether 'twas you who were there, Lorna," he said.

"Indeed, then it is," said she. "Who else would be sleeping beside you in the hearth?" And with that she got up and lit the candle. She found Owen halfway up the chimney, clinging to the stone walls, and he black with soot! He had one boot on, but the point of the other had struck Lorna, and 'twas that which woke her. Owen came down out of the chimney and washed himself, and from that time on there was no envy on him ever to have a dream again.

# The Lucky Rabbit's Foot

W HEN PEOPLE SPEAK of wizardry and spellcraft, their thoughts often turn to Scotland and the Highlands. There the summer sun shines long into the night, and magic is as common as dreaming.

And it was on such a fine summer morning that Shane Davidson, youngest son of the clan chieftain, was out hunting hares in the misty mountain meadows.

He ran a hand through his thatch of red hair, so like his father's, and took aim with his rifle at a hare who was quietly nibbling on wild carrots. He took a deep breath, steadied himself, and was about to fire, when the eyes of the silvery gray creature met his own.

For a long moment they stared at one another. Then, as quick as sunlight on water, the hare was gone, crashing through the dense grass.

Shane cursed loudly and was about to give chase when he remembered that rabbits run in circles. He hid himself in the grass and waited for the creature to return.

Sure enough, the rabbit ran right in front of him. This time he did not hesitate. Bang! The gun recoiled in his hands, and when he looked at the spot where the rabbit had been, he swore softly. He had only barely hit the creature, who had left behind as evidence a bloody right hind foot, severed at the first joint.

"Damnú air!" he sighed. "Nothing to fill the belly with. But it is not a complete loss. I shall keep the foot as a good-luck token." Carefully he wrapped the rabbit's foot in a bit of cloth and tucked it into his knapsack.

He was whistling as he came down the path, but as soon as Shane reached the door, he heard someone moaning and groaning from within. He stepped over the threshhold and there, sitting by the fire, was Maureen Dawson, his old nursemaid. The big black cat that she always kept as company rose up its back and spat at him.

"Maureen, what is it?" he asked gently. "Are you in pain?"

"Oh, me lad," she wailed, her face ashen, tears streaming down her cheeks. "I was cutting wood in the high meadow, and I accidentally struck off my own foot!"

"Oh, my Lord!" he cried, rushing to her side. He carefully took hold of her leg to tend to the bandages. "However did you get back down here? Did you...did you bring the foot with you? Perhaps the doctor..."

"No, no!" she moaned, shaking her head. "I left it where it lay."

A sneaking suspicion crept into Shane's heart. Without a word he rose and reached into his knapsack. He unwrapped the tiny bundle he had placed inside and, as he knew he would, found not a rabbit's foot, but that of a human woman. It was then that he realized the woman who had raised and tended him his entire life was in truth a witch.

# The Witch's Daughter

———◆•◆•◆———

DEVIN MACSWEENY AND his wife, Aideen, were living in Balleykeely long ago, and they had only one daughter, a young girl with the same flame red hair and golden eyes of her mother. Síbéal was the darling of the county, and no child had a sweeter nature and kinder temper than she.

One day Devin was cutting turf at Rosslare. When it

came time for the evening meal, Aideen sent her daughter with food—a hunk of soda bread, a piece of cheese, and a wooden bowl of barley broth.

"It's a fine daughter you are, surely, to bring your hungry father his food," Devin laughed and rumpled his daughter's hair. They sat down at the edge of the bog, looking out to sea, and ate their meal in comfortable silence.

"Do you see that ship?" Síbéal asked, gesturing with her empty bowl.

"The one heading from the mouth of the harbor? I do indeed," answered her father.

"Yes, the one called the Sea Queen," the girl said sweetly. "Do you ever wonder where the ships go?"

"To London town, I'd imagine. They have a fine port there," said Devin. "Why the sudden interest?"

"Oh, if I had a mind to it, the ship would never reach her goal." Síbéal shrugged and took another bite of her cheese.

"That's a horrible thing to be saying now!" cried her father. "What makes you think you can do anything to that ship, you such a small girl and the ship so far away?"

Síbéal said nothing but rose to wash her little wooden dish in the stream. "Look now, Da, and see what I can do," she called over her shoulder.

Devin was lighting his pipe but stood up and walked over to where his daughter was standing and looking out to sea.

"What nonsense are you up to, girl?" he asked suspiciously. He glanced out over the waters and saw that the ship that had been heading from the harbor's mouth was now sailing straight toward the cliffs. He saw that Síbéal was muttering strange words to herself and turning the wooden bowl around in her hand.

"And if I tip the bowl over," she said with a laugh, "the ship will do the same."

Fear and horror clutched at the farmer's heart. "Who taught you to do such a thing?" he asked in a strained voice.

"Why, Mother did, of course," Síbéal looked up in surprise. "She taught me many a fine trick."

"Why don't you let the ship go, my daughter, and let's go home."

"But you haven't finished cutting turf," protested Síbéal, but she let the ship go free, and it floated out to the open sea again.

"Nevertheless, I suddenly feel a great weariness come over me."

Devin said nothing more on the matter, neither to his daughter nor his wife. Yet that night, he cleaned and washed himself well and put on his Sunday best. He was angry and hurt to know that he had married a woman who practiced the dark arts and who had taught them to their lovely child. He left the cottage that night, taking nothing but his tools, intent on leaving them behind. Wherever he went, no one knows. He was never seen again.

# The Red Otter

ONE FROSTY AUTUMN morning Caradog and Olwen, brothers from the village of Llandrillo, were hunting for otter along the banks of a sparkling river. Hearing a rustle in the undergrowth behind them, they spun around to see something small and reddish scampering away.

"Did you see that?" Caradog asked. "What was it?"

"I didn't see it clearly, but I think it was an otter." Olwen replied. "What else would it be?"

"A fox perhaps?" Caradog mused.

"It's been a long time since a fox was seen in these parts. It's an otter, as sure as I'm born."

"Very well, then. Let's go get him."

The brothers followed the faint trail to a small hole beside the river. "There's a second hole a way's down," called Olwen.

"Good. Cover it with your sack and I'll poke a stick into this end. That'll rouse him."

So Olwen held his knapsack over one entrance, and Caradog poked his stick into the other. Before they knew it, something scuttled out into the sack. Olwen quickly closed it and grinned at his brother. "Elias Prichard is paying two pounds sterling for each otter pelt."

"Then we'll celebrate tonight at the pub."

"You're buying the first round."

Each brother grabbed an end of the sack and together they carried it back down the trail. They had not gone far when they heard a little voice say, "Oh, me! Oh, my! My mother is calling me!"

"What are you talking about?" demanded Olwen. "I don't hear Mum calling us."

"I didn't say anything," insisted Caradog. "I thought it was you."

"D-do you think it was the otter?" asked Olwen, looking at the bag fearfully.

"Of course not. Did you ever hear of an otter speaking? And what would an otter say if he could? I don't think he'd be calling for his mother."

"You're right, Caradog. It must have been the wind or something."

They set off once again for the village but had not gone much farther when they heard the tiny voice. "My mother is calling me! I must not be late for supper!"

So startled were the brothers when they realized the voice was coming from the sack that they dropped it on the ground. A little man with a tiny red cap and cloak crawled out and dusted off his pants. "I'm much obliged to you," he bowed, tipping his tiny hat in salute. "Thank you ever so much." And then he was gone as quick as, aye quicker than, a blink.

"Did you see that?" asked Caradog, dumbfounded.

"I didn't see anything," replied Olwen slowly. "Who would believe us, anyway?"

"You're right. Let's go straight to the pub. I'm buying the first round."

From that day forward, whenever the brothers went out hunting, they always checked twice before they tried to carry anything home in their bag.

# Celtic Tales Glossary

*arwn*   dear one
*avoch*   Oh, no!
*calleacha*   old woman
*canwyll gorff*   corpse candle
*ceildh*   party
*ciall agus ceol*   sense and music
*curragh*   boat, coracle
*Damnú air!*   Damn it!
*Diabhal*   Devil
*Dia dhuit.*   Hello.
*Dia is Muire dhuit.*   Hello (said in return).
*Fomorians*   race of sea robbers who were probably
   originally gods representing the powers of evil and
   darkness
*Is leat-sa so; is leam-sa sin.*   This is yours; that is mine.
*Korrigans*   faeries who live in a well
*máither*   mother
*moggie*   cat
*poítín*   moonshine, illicit whiskey
*rath*   hill
*Samhaim*   Halloween
*sheoguey*   mystical, otherworldly
*sidhe*   (1) underground fort or palace where fairies live
   (2) fairy folk of Ireland (*the sidhe* is plural)
*Tá sé fuar inniu.*   It's cold outside.
*toili*   death portent
*toleath*   sound heard before a death: sometimes a rapping, tolling of a bell, fluttering of wings, pounding
   of nails into a coffin, shuffling, or thudding
*Tuathe de Dannan*   Fair People, Faeries

# Celtic Pronunciation Guide

Here are a few simple rules to keep in mind when pronouncing Celtic names and words. Many Celtic words have the same phonetic values as English letters, with these exceptions.

| Celtic | English Equivalent | Celtic | English Equivalent |
|--------|-------------------|--------|-------------------|
| *a* | like *o* in cot | *fh* | not pronounced |
| *á* | like *aw* in paw | *g* | hard, like *g* in tiger |
| *bh* | like *v* or *w* | *gh* | like *y* |
| *c* | always hard, like *c* in cattle | *i* | like *ee* in seek |
| | | *mh* | like *v* or *w* |
| *ch* | like *ch* in Bach | *ó* | like *o* in go |
| *dh* | like *y* | *s* | like *sh* before *e* or *i* |
| *e* | not pronounced before *a* unless accented | *sh* | like *h* |
| | | *th* | like *h* |
| *é* | like *ay* in play | *ú* | like *oo* in zoo |

# Index